This book belongs to:

_____

THE NIGHT THE GRANDFATHERS DANCED

BY **Linda Theresa Raczek**

ILLUSTRATED BY **Katalin Olah Ehling**

Northland Publishing

For my sweet daughter, Autumn
—L.T.R.

To my husband, Helmut; my children, Kristina and Peter;
and to Suzanne Brown, all of whom have supported me
in all ways during my adventures in art.
—K.O.E.

The illustrations in this book were done using the batik process
The text type was set in Monotype Italian Old Style
Calligraphy by Judythe Sieck
Designed by Trina Stahl
Edited by Kathryn Wilder
Production supervision by Lisa Brownfield

Manufactured in Hong Kong by South Sea International Press Ltd.

FIRST IMPRESSION
ISBN 0-87358-610-7

Library of Congress Catalog Card Number 95-11090
Cataloging-in-Publication Data

Raczek, Linda Theresa, 1953-
The night the grandfathers danced / written by
Linda Theresa Raczek ; illustrated by Katalin Olah Ehling.
p.   cm.
"A Justin company."
Summary: When the boys her own age run away from her at the
Bear Dance, Autumn Eyetoo picks a partner from
among the old men of the tribe.
ISBN 0-87358-610-7
1. Ute Indians—Juvenile fiction. 2. Bear dance—Juvenile fiction.
[1. Ute Indians—Fiction. 2. Indians of North America—Fiction.
3. Bear dance—Fiction.] I. Ehling, Katalin Olah, 1941- ill. II. Title.
PZ7.R1115Ni 1995
[E]—dc20   95-11090

0534/7.5M/9-95

A Note from the Author

The Bear Dance came about, one story goes, because long, long ago, a bear taught a special springtime dance to a Ute hunter wandering alone in the woods. Bear, the wisest of all animals and most courageous next to Mountain Lion, is a brother to the True People (*Weeminuche,* or Ute Mountain Utes) and a bearer of magic, and so the hunter taught the dance to his people. Today, Bear Dance continues as an annual celebration of winter's passing and the reunion of families and friends.

After the first spring thunder—the sound of Bear growling deep within his den—Ute men, in honor of the women, make plans and preparations for the four-day dance. They create a six-foot brush fence of cedar boughs, bring forth the special drums and bear growlers, and prepare the feast while the women shake the wrinkles from their traditional dresses and practice dance steps.

The round, brush-enclosed dance grounds (*a-vik-wok-et,* or "cave of sticks") are modeled after Bear's den. The one opening faces east. Inside, women ask men to dance by brushing them with their shawls while the Cat Man *(moose-a-la-pete-ah)* supervises, adding humor and maintaining order with the touch of his willow whip. The line of male dancers faces east, and the women face the men.

The haunting drumming pounds deep into the heart as the songs and steps of Bear Dance pass from one generation to the next in the oldest and most unique of Ute ceremonies. On the last of the four days, the men and women separate into couples under the Cat Man's direction, and some remain together for years to come. This continues the cycle of life, love, and tradition among the True People, in a form that honors their brother, Bear, who still lives free in the mountains the Utes once called home.

Autumn Eyetoo slipped a brightly beaded barrette into her hair. Pulling her pink shawl loosely around her small shoulders, she turned toward the looking glass. Autumn smiled at what she saw.

It was to be her first *Mama'kwa'kap,* Bear Dance, and she was very proud of her new clothes. As she walked through the sagebrush to the dance grounds, Autumn felt the other children admiring her long ribbon dress and wide, beaded belt. She looked around with pleasure, taking in the rich greens and pinks that spread into the foothills of their sacred place, Sleeping Ute

Mountain. Like the bears, it lay sprawled beneath the blue sky, waiting to be awakened. Nearby, frisky ponies kicked up their heels and broke into a gallop, showering Autumn with the fresh scent of crushed sage.

The *Weenuchu,* Autumn's people, looked forward each
year to Bear Dance. It came in the spring when the earth had
warmed and the hardships of winter were fading from memory.
In the old days, it came when the people moved out of the hills,
like bears stirring from their winter dens. Now most of them
lived in modern houses, but still the ancient dance brought the
tribe together every year.

Autumn passed the wooden stands where the older people gathered to play the Ute hand games. The incense of cedar fires and simmering stews from the fry bread stands filled the air. Chubby babies nodded off in their cradleboards to the comforting sounds of laughter and song.

Finally, Autumn stood at the entrance to the big, round dance grounds, the place her people called the "cave of sticks." She squinted into the bright sunlight, looking for a place to sit in the shade of the brush wall.

"Autumn! Come here!" It was her best friend, Tasheena. Autumn joined her girlfriends on a colorful blanket spread over the hard dirt.

Now the singers stood and said a few words to everyone in Ute, the language of Autumn's people. Then they started to rub the familiar rattling rhythm on bear growlers, long notched sticks. The grating sound echoed in the drum box, sending out a message to the bears: Wake up! Come dance with us, *Kwiy'agat,* Brother Bear.

The Bear Dance had begun!

Autumn watched a funny man with a whip clown around
with the first dancers. The people called him the Cat Man.

He kept them in line and made sure a man got up to dance when a woman brushed him with her shawl.

Some old women pushed the girls playfully from behind. "Go dance," one said, laughing. "The Bear Dance will be over and you'll end up old and single like me."

Autumn blushed. She was still a young girl, and had no plans to get married yet. But she did have her eye on a boy her age. When the first song ended, she jumped up and went to touch the boy with her shawl. But he saw her coming and took off at a run—out of reach of the Cat Man.

Autumn's heart sank. She so wanted to join the long line of dancers. Clouds of dust puffed up from their feet as the singing and rhythm filled the air once again. Her feet practiced tiny steps. Some of the young men had two partners, one on each arm. They danced with big smiles on their faces, their braids flying. It just wasn't fair!

Autumn and the other girls sat under the hot sun all afternoon. They watched the boys run, yelling and laughing, through the shade of the fry bread stands. The beautiful clothes she had been so proud of now felt dusty and hot.

Finally, the sun sank behind the mountain and cast long, cool shadows. For the first time, Autumn noticed a few men who had not been asked to dance all day. They were the very old men of the tribe, with dark, wrinkled eyes, and long, gray braids. She touched Tasheena's hand and smiled. "If the boys will not dance with us, what an honor it would be to dance with one of the grandfathers. I dare you!"

Tasheena's eyes opened wide. "No one ever dances with those old men!" she said. Some of the other girls giggled at the thought.

Autumn faced them with fierce eyes. Without a word, she rose to her feet and walked across the dance circle.

She stood before the first old man. He stared ahead, unseeing, his eyes milky blue. "I hear you are a wonderful dancer, Grandfather," Autumn said, touching him with a swish of her shawl.

The old man smiled slowly. "It has been a long time since these eyes have seen much, but my feet remember plenty," he said. Autumn took his hand and led him toward the line of dancers. As they stepped into place, the other girls followed, each walking gently beside one of the old men.

Autumn Eyetoo looked up and saw a pale sliver of a
moon, like the claw of a bear, slip out from behind the clouds.
She smiled as the bear growlers sent their call into the night.
Her first Bear Dance had begun—the one her people would
remember as The Night the Grandfathers Danced.

About the Author

Linda Theresa Raczek lives in a turn-of-the-century Colorado home near the Four Corners area. She loves to garden, and her many trees, shrubs, and flowers once attracted a wayward moose into her yard to graze. Linda has worked as a naturalist, sailor, social worker, and as the children's attorney for the Ute Mountain Ute tribe. She now divides her time between writing and caring for her young daughter and their old dog, who is 105—in dog years, of course. Linda's fiction and nonfiction have appeared in many children's and young adult magazines, and a story of hers appears in Northland's anthology *Walking the Twilight: Women Writers of the Southwest*. *The Night the Grandfathers Danced* is her first children's book.

About the Illustrator

Katalin Olah Ehling was born in Hungary in 1941, and moved from war-torn Germany to the United States in 1950. She received her art education at the American Academy of Art in Chicago, L'Ecole de Dessin de la Mode du Mademoiselle Boizot in Paris, France, and Phoenix College in Arizona. She discovered batik in the late 1960s, and was immediately hooked; currently she batiks, draws, and paints. A resident of Arizona since 1968, Katalin's subject matter is largely the people and places of the Southwest. She finds the Southwest similar to the Old World where people also live close to the land. Her first children's book illustrations appear in *The Night the Grandfathers Danced*.